westermann

W0351986

CAMDEN TOWN

Vocab Practice 9

Erarbeitet von

Tanja Mees

Liebe Schülerin, lieber Schüler,

wer eine fremde Sprache lernt, will andere Menschen verstehen können und von ihnen verstanden werden. Je mehr Wörter und Wendungen du in einer Fremdsprache kennst und verwenden kannst, desto besser wirst du dich verständigen können. Übung macht den Meister, und mit *Vocab Practice* kannst du deinen Wortschatz ständig erweitern und festigen.

Zu jedem *Theme* deines Textbooks findest du in *Vocab Practice* viele verschiedene Aufgaben und spannende Rätsel. In den *Check your vocab*-Aufgaben auf den Seiten 12, 23, 35 und 47 kannst du eine Auswahl wichtiger Vokabeln aus jedem *Theme* trainieren. Neue englische Wörter und Wendungen, die dir im Unterricht, in deinem Textbook oder anderswo begegnen, kannst du auf den Seiten 13, 24, 36 und 48 unter *MY words* notieren und ordnen. Nach und nach ergänzt du dann diese Sammlungen, so dass du am Ende ein ganz persönliches Wörterbuch hast, in dem du immer wieder nachschlagen kannst.

Lerntipps und Hinweise ! unterstützen dich beim Wortschatztraining.

Du kannst mit *Vocab Practice* selbstständig zu Hause arbeiten. Mit den Lösungen im beiliegenden Heft überprüfst du deine Antworten.

Viel Spaß und Erfolg mit *Vocab Practice*!

Bildquellen

|Alamy Stock Photo (RMB), Abingdon/Oxfordshire: Ball, David 6.1; Cultura RM 10.1; Gordon, Paul Christian 27.1; Pictorial Press Ltd 3.2; Shore, Enrique 33.1. |fotolia.com, New York: PIXATERRA 5.1. |iStockphoto.com, Calgary: Brainsil Titel; Freder, Dirk 8.1; giftlegacy 26.2; inhauscreative 9.1; narvikk 12.1; oatawa 34.1; omersukrugoksu 3.1, 13.1; patpitchaya 21.1, 44.1; SolStock 4.1; spyarm 15.1. |Marckwort, Ulf, Kassel: 16.1. |Shutterstock.com, New York: alex.zvar93 46.1; Bparsons98 14.1; Cast Of Thousands 47.1, 48.1; Ground Picture 7.1; Kongpraphat 30.1; rommma 24.1; Sergeeva, Leka 42.1; Song_about_summer 26.1; Tharun 15 10.2, 23.1, 23.2, 23.3; Tote 19.1. |stock.adobe.com, Dublin: C. Schüßler 17.1, 45.1; cpask Titel; DDRockstar 38.1, 38.2; doomu 20.1; klyaksun 28.1; maglara 31.1; momius 41.1; Nieschefart 18.1; sassenfeld 35.1; strichfiguren 36.1; Vitaliy 39.1; wildworx 22.1.

1 Word search

a) Find the English words for the following German words in the word search. Circle them. ↓ → ↗ ↘

Aussöhnung • *Australier/in* • *einheimisch* • *eingeboren* • *(Kultur)Erbe* • *Glaube* • *Identität* • *Kolonie* • *Kolonisation* • *Stolz* • *Werk* • *Wut*

A	A	U	S	T	R	A	L	I	A	N	S	O	R
L	A	A	N	I	T	I	N	C	V	I	N	N	E
Z	C	T	I	T	E	O	O	D	I	C	A	I	C
Y	R	O	G	O	I	A	N	E	R	H	T	D	O
O	O	I	L	T	H	E	N	R	I	I	I	E	N
L	R	R	A	O	S	E	I	G	I	N	V	N	C
P	T	E	N	R	N	I	R	N	E	A	E	T	I
I	R	O	T	I	N	I	Y	I	G	R	Y	I	L
C	O	L	O	N	Y	D	Z	S	T	N	E	T	I
L	N	Y	A	D	U	R	T	A	I	A	T	Y	A
O	P	R	I	D	E	W	Y	O	T	N	G	V	T
H	A	I	I	E	C	I	A	N	X	I	E	E	I
T	I	N	D	I	G	E	N	O	U	S	O	I	O
R	E	L	I	G	I	O	N	I	R	I	O	N	N

b) Match the right words from a) with the definitions. For one item there is more than one solution.

1 the act of making something new: ______________________

2 a country or an area which is ruled by people from another country: ______________________

3 the end of a conflict and the start of a new and better relationship: ______________________

4 the belief that a god or multiple gods exist: ______________________

5 having lived in a placed long before other people came to live there: ______________________

6 Where you were born and where you live, are parts of your ______________________.

7 a strong feeling you have, when you think something is unfair or bad: ______________________

8 a feeling you have when you did something really well or something went really well: ______________________

9 when another country takes control of a country and sends its own people to live and rule there: ______________________

2 Adjectives and adverbs

a) Write down the words.

1 /ə'fɪʃ(ə)l/ ____________

2 /'gɪlti/ ____________

3 /kri'eɪtɪv/ ____________

4 /'trɒpɪk(ə)l/ ____________

5 /ˌəʊvə'kraʊdɪd/ ____________

6 /'taɪni/ ____________

7 /'præktɪk(ə)l/ ____________

8 /'fɒrɪn/ ____________

9 /'preʃəs/ ____________

10 /strest/ ____________

11 /di:p/ ____________

12 /'keɪpəb(ə)l/ ____________

b) Complete the sentences with some of the words from a).

1 Jack is ____________ of speaking three languages.

2 Charlotte felt ____________ after eating all the cookies.

3 Popular sites like Uluru are often ____________ by tourists.

4 English, Māori and New Zealand Sign Language are the three ____________ languages of New Zealand.

5 A school uniform can be quite ____________ as you don't have to think about what to wear to school.

6 Compared to elephants, mice are ____________ animals.

7 A lot of people feel ____________ when they have too much work to do.

8 Harper is a ____________ person. She always writes new stories.

3 Word game

For each category, find words that start with the given letters.

	noun	verb	adjective	adverb
P	*pride*	*profit from*	*precious*	*properly*
E				
T				
F				
C				

4 The platypus

a) Complete the sentences with the correct words.

capable • native • possibly • raises (2×) • related • severe • tiny • unsure

egg-laying mammal – *Eier legendes Säugetier*
hatch – *schlüpfen*

Kangaroos and koala bears are 1 ______________ the most famous Australian animals. But they are of course not the only 2 ______________ animals. Another one of them is called platypus and it looks rather special.

When the first Europeans saw a dead platypus in 1799, they were 3 ______________ if it was a real animal.

The platypus is an egg-laying mammal and not 4 ______________ to any other kind of living animal. It lives alone in lakes or rivers in the eastern part of Australia and is an excellent swimmer. Platypuses are 5 ______________ of staying under water for up to two minutes and eat small water animals. The male produces a venom that causes 6 ______________ pain. Scientists believe that the venom is mostly used in fights with other males. The female platypus usually 7 ______________ two babies. First, it lays two 8 ______________ eggs and keeps them warm for ten days. After the babies have hatched, they will drink their mother's milk for about four months. The female 9 ______________ the babies on her own.

Platypuses are long-lived animals, living up to 20 years both in the wild and in captivity.

b) How much can you remember? Try to answer the questions without looking at the text.

1 What did the Europeans think about the platypus when they saw it for the first time?

____

2 Where does the platypus live?

____

3 What is special about the animal?

____

4 How many babies does a female platypus raise?

____

5 Nouns, nouns, nouns

Do the crossword.

Down ↓

1 an area with a lot of trees and a lot of rain
3 After the ... the castle looked as good as new.
7 It's no ... that so many people visit Uluru every year. It's a beautiful site.
8 The ... of water and air is a huge problem.
9 a kind of celebration
11 Heat can do a lot of ... to the environment.
15 It is a ... that they were so young when they died.
17 You need to have a ... to drive a car.
18 All the people living together are the ...
21 The land was under British ...

Across →

2 Hundreds of people joined the protest ...
4 The new yellow ... on the wall looks lovely.
5 It's amazing how much ... Ruby has about fish.
6 It is important to know that you and your work have a ....
9 Aboriginal Australians feel a close ... with the land they live in.
10 The whole team felt a ... of pride after they had won the competition.
12 Jake drank his lemonade through a ...
13 The ... cheered when the politician came on stage.
14 Josh and Mia love hiking because then they can experience the ... of nature.
16 Climate change is a ... for a lot of animals.
18 The new king gave his first ...
19 The Australian Museum has a famous ... of Aboriginal art.
20 It is often difficult to break a ... and change things.
22 I am sorry but I will not make an ... for you.

6 What fits together?

a) Pick one part from each box to make verbs. Write them down. Use each part only once.

abo • ana • bene • commu • con • pub • re • repre • suf • va	fer • fit • flect • lish • lish • lyse • nicate • ry • sent • tain

____

____

____

____

____

b) Complete the sentences with the correct forms of the verbs from a).

1 Thea and her friends ______________ everyday by text.

2 I need more time to ______________ before I can make a decision.

3 The author ______________ their last book five years ago.

4 Levi hates to see animals ______________.

5 The athletes feel proud to ______________ their country at the competitions.

6 Please ______________ the interview and write down the most important information.

7 In the United States, slavery was ______________ in 1865.

8 Students can greatly ______________ from an exchange in a foreign country.

9 Your text will be more interesting when you ______________ the sentence structure.

10 The box ______________ all the letters she had ever written.

7 Words without vowels

Complete the words without vowels.

1 James ___v___rc___m___ his fear of h___ ___ghts and started h___k___ng in the m___ ___nt___ ___ns.

2 P___rs___n___lly, I have never been to a r___ ___nf___r___st.

3 Using plastic pl___t___s and str___ws is not ___nv___r___nm___nt___lly fr___ ___ndly.

4 Australia is a m___lt___c___lt___r___l s___c___ ___ty.

8 Word families

Complete the sentences with another word from the same word family.

1 Mark was amazed when he first saw how fast a kangaroo could hop. He thinks they are ____________ animals.

2 The hockey team was proud of their success. They all felt a sense of ____________ that they had won the competition.

3 There is no big difference between the two cakes. They only ____________ in size.

4 We still don't know the identity of the person who was killed. The police will do their best to ____________ them as soon as possible.

5 It is a crime to steal somebody's mobile phone. Jack the Ripper was a well-known ____________ who murdered five women.

6 The topics of the presentations are really diverse and there is a great ____________ of opinions on some of the topics.

7 My neighbour's dog is very friendly. The dog even has a very special ____________ with my cat.

8 You have to be careful when you go swimming near the rocks, it can be dangerous. Often people get injured because they didn't take enough ____________.

9 Word trios

a) Sort the words into groups of three.

communicate • harm • message • multicultural • plate • pollution • society • straw

1	2	3	4
glass	phone	diversity	environment

b) Make one or two sentences with the each of the groups.

1 ____________

2 ____________

3 ____________

4 ____________

10 Say it in English – talking about the environment

Write down the sentences in English.

Remember that you don't have to translate word for word. !

1 Wir müssen die Schönheit der Natur beschützen.

2 Die tropischen Regenwälder sind in Gefahr.

3 Fische leiden unter hohen Wassertemperaturen.

4 Um die Umwelt zu schützen, sind Strohhalme und Teller aus Plastik verboten.

5 Viele Menschen protestieren gegen die Zerstörung der Umwelt.

6 Zu viel Tourismus, zum Beispiel an Stränden und in den Bergen, kann die Natur zerstören.

7 Der Klimawandel ist die Hauptursache für extremes Wetter.

8 Naturkatastrophen, wie zum Beispiel schwere Überflutungen oder Tornados, kommen immer häufiger vor.

9 Es ist noch nicht zu spät, um etwas gegen den Klimawandel zu tun.

11 Connectives and conjunctions

a) Complete the sentences with the correct word.

1 Charlotte checked her phone for messages. ______________ (Meanwhile/Since) her cat jumped on the table.

2 ______________ (Although/Until) Kylie has never been to Tasmania yet, she is absolutely sure that she will love it there.

3 Oliver wants to make a cake right now, ______________ (as/however), he is still shopping.

4 Willow won the swimming competition, ______________ (whereas/even though) she didn't feel well.

5 ______________ (Because/As soon as) I get home I will take a shower.

6 Ethan acted ______________ (as if/although) he hadn't met Mia before.

7 ______________ (After/Before) several days with lots of rain, the weather finally changed.

8 ______________ (As/Although) Jack loves to play hockey himself, he is not really interested in watching it on TV.

b) Match the English words with the German meaning. Draw lines.

1 so	A bis
2 as	B wo(hin)gegen
3 since	C obwohl
4 whereas	D damit
5 even though	E weil
6 until	F während

c) Write a sentence with each of the words from b).

____

____

____

____

12 Phrases

These phrases are mixed up. Sort them and write them down.

gain a novel	publish plastic	ban the necessary information
get back from a certain topic	attach experience	specialize in difficulties
overcome a photo	learn school	contains a foreign language

publish a novel

13 Do you know the words?

Fill in the grid.

		your own definition of the word	a sentence with the word
→	cycle	*a number of events that happen in the same order again and again*	*Farmers live with the cycle of the seasons.*
1	harm		
2	licence		
3	tragedy		
4	exception		
5	rainforest		
6	speech		

14 Check your vocab

Fill in the right words. Be careful to use the right form of the words.

according to • as • be based on • contain • currently • despite • float • foreign • get back • just • meanwhile • no matter • overcome • possibly • be related to • represent • run • sign up for • specialize • take a risk

1 Many of her problems ______________________ too much stress.

2 ______________________ I left the house, it started to rain.

3 ______________________ statistics temperatures have risen in the last years.

4 The novel ______________________ a true story.

5 Ben finally ______________________ his fear of spiders.

6 Could we ______________________ change the topic of the presentation?

7 We all want to live in a ______________________ society.

8 ______________________ the bad weather, the trip was great.

9 Jon is ______________________ looking for a job.

10 The book ______________________ all the poems by William Shakespeare.

11 A lot of plastic ______________________ on the sea.

12 Sometimes you have to ______________________.

13 Yesterday, ______________________ I from Sydney.

14 Oscar and Leo want to ______________________ the music club.

15 Call me when you get there, ______________________ how late it is.

16 Liam likes to learn ______________________ languages.

17 I will write the texts. ______________________ you can look for photos for our presentation.

18 The shop ______________________ in coffee and chocolate.

19 The collection ______________________ the most important Australian artists.

20 Parramatta River ______________________ through Sydney and is part of Port Jackson, the natural harbour of Sydney.

15 MY words – Australia

On this page you can collect words and phrases to talk about Australia.

> You can always come back to this page and add new words and phrases. !

Australian history

one of the oldest living civilizations

Society in Australia

fight for equal rights

School in Australia

wide range of electives

Australian English

g'day, no worries

1 Hidden phrases

a) Find the way through the maze[1] and write down the phrases hidden in the maze.
Start at the →

1 maze – *Irrgarten*

S	O	T	O	D	O	S	O	M	E	T	H	I	D	O	W	T	D	E	P	P	U	P	P	O
O	D	D	D	O	S	O	M	E	I	N	G	C	E	D	O	D	E	S	O	U	S	U	O	S
T	O	E	O	M	O	M	E	T	H	I	N	O	M	E	D	I	U	S	U	B	E	S	P	O
D	T	S	O	E	M	E	T	H	I	N	G	C	O	M	E	W	S	E	B	G	B	E	P	P
E	S	O	C	T	E	T	H	I	C	G	C	O	M	E	W	D	E	B	G	N	G	B	U	P
D	O	P	G	N	T	H	I	N	G	C	O	H	I	W	D	E	N	G	N	I	N	G	S	E
O	P	P	P	I	H	I	N	G	C	O	M	T	W	D	E	N	R	N	I	H	I	N	G	B
U	S	U	P	N	I	N	G	M	E	D	O	E	D	E	N	R	E	I	H	T	H	I	N	G
→ B	E	S	M	O	N	G	C	O	M	E	E	M	O	N	R	E	C	E	T	E	S	H	T	I
U	S	T	O	C	G	C	O	M	E	D	O	O	S	R	E	C	N	R	E	M	O	S	I	W
O	T	N	W	O	C	E	M	E	T	O	O	S	H	E	C	N	O	N	C	E	R	N	E	D
S	O	T	H	D	O	M	N	W	N	T	T	I	T	C	N	O	C	O	E	R	N	E	I	T
O	M	E	T	E	M	E	D	O	W	T	I	W	I	N	O	C	E	C	R	E	E	D	W	I
G	N	I	H	D	E	D	O	W	W	I	W	P	W	I	C	E	B	E	C	N	D	A	I	T
A	S	N	I	S	S	E	B	N	P	U	E	U	P	W	O	C	T	B	O	N	A	G	A	I
S	F	A	R	A	S	M	E	E	M	O	M	E	U	I	B	T	S	T	I	C	G	A	G	A
S	A	R	M	O	S	O	B	M	O	C	O	W	P	T	E	B	N	S	A	G	A	E	A	G
S	S	A	E	M	E	M	E	B	C	D	S	H	W	I	S	N	I	A	G	A	E	T	E	A
O	S	S	B	E	B	Y	D	E	N	E	H	T	I	S	N	I	A	G	A	E	T	A	T	A
C	Y	D	O	B	O	D	Y	N	R	D	S	H	T	H	I	A	G	A	E	T	A	N	I	N
S	I	Y	D	O	D	Y	N	R	E	M	O	S	H	M	D	G	D	I	S	C	R	I	M	A
C	S	I	Y	D	S	C	O	E	C	E	M	O	S	O	I	N	G	D	C	R	I	N	I	N
O	C	S	I	Y	I	S	C	O	N	C	E	M	O	M	H	I	D	I	R	I	M	I	N	A
N	O	C	S	I	S	C	C	N	C	E	I	E	M	E	T	H	I	D	I	M	I	N	E	T

1 ____________________

2 ____________________

3 ____________________

4 ____________________

5 ____________________

6 ____________________

b) Make sure you know the meaning of each phrase and write a sentence with each of them.

2 In a debate

Complete the sentences. Write down the German phrases in English. Be careful to use the right form of the phrases.

1 Going by train is environmentally friendly ______________ (*im Gegensatz zu*) going by plane.

2 Sienna ______________ (*vorbringen*) a very important question.

3 ______________ (*Wie ich es sehe*), alcohol is a dangerous drug.

4 ______________ (*Meiner Meinung nach*), teenagers shouldn't be allowed to drink or smoke.

5 Leo ______________ (*behaupten*) that we are not able to protect the environment.

6 I ______________ (*für meinen Teil*) love to go by bike everywhere but there are many people who think it is more comfortable to go by car.

7 ______________ (*Ehrlich gesagt*), I sometimes think that nothing will change.

8 ______________ (*Ich verstehe, was du meinst*) but I don't agree with you.

3 Missing letters

a) Complete the words.

1 co_____unicate	5 obse_____ive	9 mi_____information
2 a_____ear	6 self-est_____m	10 am_____sed
3 rev_____l	7 a_____icted	11 humor_____s
4 acce_____	8 sar_____astic	12 spe_____ific

b) Complete the sentences with some of the words from a).

1 Sometimes people become ______________ users of social media.

2 Everybody laughed when Harper described the holiday in Italy in a really ______________ way.

3 Please, give more ______________ information about the dangers of taking drugs.

4 It is important to prevent teenagers from having ______________ to drugs.

5 A low ______________ can be a big problem.

6 Suddenly, a cat ______________ behind the tree.

7 Eden's father has been ______________ to alcohol for years.

8 At the party, Levi ______________ that he will move from Chicago to New York.

4 Nouns

Write down the words. Be careful to write them on the correct side.

										1	C	O	W							
										2				T						
						S				3			U							
					U					4				W						
				E						5			B							
					T					6			J							
						T				7		R								
							I			8			L							

1 an animal that lives on a farm – That is an interesting ... chart!
2 The ... of the film was really confusing. – something you can smoke or drink that makes you addicted
3 Please, tell me the ...! – an important topic
4 You have to press the ... to open the door. – After the training, everybody needs to take a ...
5 You have chosen a very interesting ... for the debate. – the place where a film or story takes place
6 the largest part of a group of things or people – It's not a big ... from my home to my best friend's home.
7 Ben had a ... when his parents suddenly died in a car accident. – a shop where you can buy medicine
8 We are allowed to use a ... in the maths exam. – There is a ... between climate change and the changes in the weather.

5 Do you know the words?

a) Write down the words.

1 ______________
2 ______________
3 ______________
4 ______________
5 ______________ (tip: it's inside)
6 ______________
7 ______________
8 ______________

b) Use the right form of the words from a) to complete the sentences. Use each word only once.

1 Using drugs like alcohol or cigarettes can damage your ______________.

2 Coen's ______________ hurt because the music was so loud.

3 When Sophie opened her ______________ again, she couldn't believe what she saw.

4 Mason hit his ______________ when he fell from his bike and had to see a doctor.

5 Lily's ______________ fell open when she saw all the presents.

6 Noah was so embarrassed that his ______________ turned red.

7 I need to get my ______________ cut. It has grown too long.

8 Rose covered her ______________ when she took out the rubbish.

6 Paraphrasing

Rewrite the sentences. There are two more words than you need.

appeal • associate • consume • contain • convey • figure out • rely on • respond to • stare at • vary

> Paraphrasing the information you have found during research is important for presentations or longer texts. !

1 This cake was made with nuts.

2 There is so much information about the phone on this page but where is the price?

3 I have never thought of social media when people talk about addictions.

4 Matilda always tries to answer her messages immediately.

5 Charlie likes basketball a lot because she loves to play in a team.

6 Theo didn't understand one word when he looked at the exercises.

7 Last week apples were quite cheap. Today they are really expensive.

8 Riley cannot get to school without her bike.

7 Odd one out

a) Circle the odd one out and write down the German meaning.

→ slowly • daily • often • never — *langsam*

1 depressed • smart • pessimistic • sad

2 entirely • completely • totally • by half

3 button • drugstore • supermarket • pharmacy

4 setting • plot • solution • story

b) Write a sentence with each of the odd words.

→ *Kenzo slowly climbed the stairs.*

8 Plural or no plural?

writer device smoking source party
attention access misinformation condition
case pharmacy reader bullying
self-esteem illness wall extract
body language

Make sure that you know whether a noun has a plural. There are also nouns that are only used in the plural, e.g. stairs.

a) Which nouns in the box have no plural? Circle them and write them down.

____

____

b) Write down the plural forms of the other nouns.

____

____

9 Scrambled words

a) Unscramble the words and write them down.

1 INLOGV ________
2 TFUHGHTOUL ________
3 SRAMT ________
4 TIOUNCHG ________
5 LLADUAYGR ________
6 ROUSMOHU ________
7 CASSTICAR ________
8 RCIH ________

b) Complete the sentences with the correct form of some of the words from a).

1 The percentage of people with a driver's licence ________ decreased between 1983 and 2018.
2 "I absolutely love this kind of weather!" Sora said ________ when she got into heavy rain.
3 They sat in ________ silence after they had searched for their dog for two hours.
4 "It was not very ________ of you to drop your phone into the toilet!"
5 Max's account of his trip to London was really ________.
6 Elon Musk is one of the ________ men in the world.

10 A cartoon

Look at the cartoon and read the text. Answer the questions.

The cartoon deals with the issue of climate change.
It shows three tiny islands in the sea. On each of the islands is a palm tree and a man. The weather on all three islands is different: there is sunshine, snow and rain.
The man on sunshine island stands under the tree, wears only short shorts and holds a drink in one hand. He appears to be very pleased with his situation.
The man on snowy island is sitting under the palm tree and wears a woolen hat, a sweater and jeans. He has snow on his nose and his body language suggests that he is cold and annoyed.
The man on rainy island also sits under the tree and wears shorts and a sleeveless[1] shirt. He tries to hide from the rain under a piece of paper. His facial expression shows that he, too, is really annoyed about the weather.
The man on the island with the sunshine says: "Climate Change? I have no idea what that means."
The aim of the cartoon might be to raise awareness to the fact that climate change is happening even if we think the weather is quite nice. To me, the cartoon is more thought-provoking than funny as it suggests that people do not understand the danger of climate change as long as the weather is fine.

1 sleeveless – *ärmellos*

1 Look at the first sentence. Write down another way of saying what the cartoon is about.

2 Find three phrases that describe how you think people feel. Write them down.

3 Write a definition for

body language

facial expression

4 What do you think about the cartoon? Do you find it funny? Write down your opinion.

11 A film review

a) Match the English and the German phrases. Draw lines. There are more German phrases than you need.

1 sadly the main actor is very unconvincing
2 the plot is complicated and hard to follow
3 the atmosphere is dark and pessimistic
4 the music creates a hopeful atmosphere
5 the film is very touching and humorous
6 the film was directed by a famous team of brothers

A Regie führte ein berühmtes Bruderpaar
B die Atmosphäre ist düster und pessimistisch
C der Film ist sehr bewegend und humorvoll
D der Hauptdarsteller ist sehr überzeugend
E das Ende ist unrealistisch und kitschig
F der Hauptdarsteller ist leider nicht überzeugend
G die Musik erzeugt eine hoffnungsvolle Atmosphäre
H es ist schwer der komplizierten Handlung zu folgen

b) Write down the sentences in English.

! Remember that it is not important to translate the sentences word for word.

→ Die Handlung ist überzeugend und die Figuren sind realistisch.

The plot is convincing and the characters are realistic.

1 Der Film spricht vor allem ein jüngeres Publikum an.

2 Das Ende ist wenig überraschend und eher langweilig.

3 Das Publikum des Films war vom ersten Moment an gefesselt.

4 Alle Schauspieler sind gut, aber der Hauptdarsteller war hervorragend.

5 Die Musik hat den Film noch furchterregender gemacht als er ohnehin ist.

6 Am Anfang ist es ziemlich schwierig der Handlung zu folgen.

7 Ich empfehle den Film allen, die sich für Geschichte interessieren.

12 Mental health

Complete the sentences.

You can look up the English sounds in your textbook on page 281. **!**

1 Ava is too ____________________ /ˌselfˈsentəd/ to care much about anybody else.

2 Because of his ____________________ /ˈɪlnəs/, Henry cannot go to school next week.

3 I need to go to the ____________________ /ˈfɑːməsi/ to buy some medicine.

4 Pippa likes the sound of her voice and has a high ____________________ /ˌself‿ɪˈstiːm/.

5 Ethan has become really ____________________ /əbˈsesɪv/ about his grades.

6 Farid always feels ____________________ /ˈæŋkʃəs/ when his friends drink a lot of alcohol.

7 Aaliyah had a nervous ____________________ /ˈbreɪkˌdaʊn/ when her brother died in an accident.

8 Social media can make people ____________________ /dɪˈprest/.

13 Verbs

a) Find eleven verbs in the word search. Circle them. ↓ →

W	O	N	D	G	V	J	S	T	A	R	E	Y	W
M	A	P	P	E	A	R	V	Y	J	Y	F	T	Y
W	X	Z	V	Y	X	R	D	T	U	N	U	Y	E
S	D	R	X	R	E	S	P	O	N	D	V	D	E
V	E	Z	R	Q	L	Y	K	K	J	I	K	L	R
A	F	M	W	U	Z	E	D	E	L	E	T	E	C
O	I	Y	V	J	G	I	Y	V	S	T	C	D	R
F	N	F	B	A	N	A	L	Y	S	E	H	X	E
A	E	E	C	X	S	U	Q	T	F	P	L	P	N
D	W	I	D	C	O	N	C	L	U	D	E	Y	U
K	E	Q	N	P	G	T	K	G	I	J	J	P	T
P	O	K	R	E	J	E	C	T	P	P	U	S	H
A	C	E	D	C	L	Q	X	X	V	Y	P	R	X
E	R	A	I	S	E	L	H	C	L	A	I	M	T

b) Complete the sentences with the correct form of some of the words from a).

1 Oh no! I've just ____________________ all my photos!

2 I don't want to be ____________________ by my illness.

3 She ____________________ any kind of help.

4 They ____________________ at each other for a long time.

5 I still have to ____________________ to your last email.

6 He ____________________ the door wide open to let some fresh air in.

14 More nouns

a) Complete the sentences with the right form of the nouns. There are more words than you need.

account • bathroom • bullying • button • brain • case • condition • device • drug • drugstore • misinformation • walls

1 My ____________ was too tired to figure out the solution to the problem.

2 There is a ____________ missing on your coat.

3 Tom has a ____________ which makes it impossible for him to become a pilot.

4 A lot of ____________ is being shared on social media.

5 ____________ is a huge problem on many schools.

6 You will have to leave tablets and other ____________ in your bags.

7 Mia painted the ____________ in her room.

8 Alcohol is a ____________ that many people consume.

b) Write a sentence with the words you did not use in a).

____

____

____

____

15 Phrases

Draw lines to make phrases.
Match the words on the left with the words on the right.

You can easily improve your English if you learn phrases instead of single words.

1 raise	A convey a feeling
2 sth has been accidentally	B appear
3 gradually	C deleted
4 analyse	D performance
5 suddenly	E an important question
6 a convincing	F attention to sth
7 try to	G the reasons
8 turn your	H improve

16 Check your vocab

Fill in the right words. Be careful to write down the correct form of the words.

attention • *besides* • *by* • *by half* • *claim* • *convey* • *convincing* • *define* • *despite* • *entirely* • *extract* • *figure out* • *gradually* • *in conclusion* • *in particular* • *issue* • *on purpose* • *personally* • *purpose* • *source* • *the ... the* • *throughout* • *truth* • *vary*

1 He ____________________ got better in History.

2 Social media can be a ____________________ of hate.

3 I am not ____________________ sure how this works.

4 You did that ____________________ !

5 We went hiking ____________________ the rain.

6 She loves graphic novels ____________________.

7 He didn't drink anything ____________________ the whole day.

8 I am not hungry. ____________________ I hate broccoli.

9 I need to ____________________ how to get from London to Edinburgh by train.

10 The house ____________________ the river is beautiful.

11 ____________________, we need to do more to protect the planet.

12 ____________________, I prefer going by bike to school.

13 I cannot ____________________ how much that means to me.

14 The ending is very ____________________ and realistic.

15 Her time online went down ____________________.

16 Remember the ____________________ of the text.

17 A text sounds more interesting when you ____________________ the sentence structure.

18 From the first page, the writer had the reader's full ____________________.

19 Please ____________________ what *bullying* is.

20 ____________________ more I think about it, ____________________ better I like the idea.

21 Eliah ____________________ that nobody told him about the new date for the presentation.

22 I still have to read the ____________________ from the novel.

23 Children's rights is a very important ____________________ that needs to be talked about.

24 Please don't make up some story, tell me the ____________________.

17 MY words – statistics

On this page you can collect words and phrases you can use when you want to talk about statistics. You can always come back later and add more words to it.

graphs and charts

line graph

describing figures

After 2022 the numbers decreased …

1 What does it mean?

a) Match the definitions with the correct words. Draw lines.

Definitions	Words	Definitions
a part of a text	identity	a person who helps a party or a group of people
people living together	attention	the description of a number of events
a situation in which people are angry with each other because they have different opinions	extract	why a person does something
an action which has a certain aim, e.g. to prevent something from happening	threat	who or what somebody is
listening to, looking at or watching something carefully	measure	when you tell somebody, you will harm them when they do not do what you want
	supporter	
	motivation	
	confrontation	
	narrative	
	society	

b) Complete the sentences with some of the words from a). Be careful to use the right form.

→ It is very easy to use a false *identity* when you are online.

1 Read the short ______________ on page three and say what it is about.

2 You need to give the book your undivided ______________.

3 Last evening there was a serious ______________ between two groups of teenagers.

4 Mila and Isaac are active ______________ of a group which fights for the rights of children.

5 We need to take appropriate ______________ to solve the problem.

6 Sometimes politicians receive terrible ______________ when they make unpopular decisions.

c) Write down the adjectives and nouns from b).

→ *false identity*

1 ______________

2 ______________

3 ______________

4 ______________

5 ______________

6 ______________

Nouns are often used with certain adjectives. Your English will sound more natural if you learn these combinations like regular vocabulary.

2 Nouns, nouns, nouns

a) Do the crossword.

Across →

1 Sam is an American. He is a ... of the United States.
2 the opposite of *life*
5 a rule that limits what you can do or what can happen
7 Emails are a very fast ... of communication.
9 a promise that something will happen
12 The US ... protects the people's right to own a gun.
14 Every person has the right to be protected from ...
15 someone who is a member of a government
18 a group of people who have joined together
22 You need the right ... to be able to do this job.
23 an organized walk

Lösungen zu Vocab Practice 9 (978-3-14-149242-2)

Theme 1: Australia

1 Word search: a)

A	A	U	S	T	R	A	L	I	A	N	S	O	R
L	A	A	N	I	T	I	N	C	V	I	N	N	E
Z	C	T	I	T	E	O	O	D	I	C	A	I	C
Y	R	O	G	O	I	A	N	E	R	H	T	D	O
O	O	I	L	T	H	E	N	R	I	I	I	E	N
L	R	R	A	O	S	E	I	G	I	N	V	N	C
P	T	E	N	R	N	I	R	N	E	A	E	T	I
I	R	O	T	I	N	I	Y	I	G	R	Y	I	L
C	O	L	O	N	Y	D	Z	S	T	N	E	T	I
L	N	Y	A	D	U	R	T	A	I	A	T	Y	A
O	P	R	I	D	E	W	Y	O	T	N	G	V	T
H	A	I	I	E	C	I	A	N	X	I	E	E	I
T	I	N	D	I	G	E	N	O	U	S	O	I	O
R	E	L	I	G	I	O	N	I	R	I	O	N	N

b) 1 creation 2 colony 3 reconciliation 4 religion 5 native/indigenous 6 heritage 7 anger 8 pride 9 colonization

2 Adjectives and adverbs: a) 1 official 2 guilty 3 creative 4 tropical 5 overcrowded 6 tiny 7 practical 8 foreign 9 precious 10 stressed 11 deep 12 capable **b)** 1 capable 2 guilty 3 overcrowded 4 official 5 practical 6 tiny 7 stressed 8 creative

3 Word game: (*Individuelle Lösungen; Lösungsvorschlag*) E elephant, eat, eager, equally T tourist, think, tropical, truly F fear, feel, foreign, fast C colony, compare, creative, clearly

4 The platypus: a) 1 possibly 2 native 3 unsure 4 related 5 capable 6 severe 7 raises 8 tiny 9 raises **b)** 1 They didn't think it was a real animal. 2 It lives in rivers and lakes in eastern Australia. 3 It lays eggs but the babies drink their mother's milk. The platypus can stay under water for two minutes and the males have a venom. 4 It raises usually two babies.

5 Nouns, nouns, nouns: Down: 1 rainforest 3 restoration 7 wonder 8 pollution 9 ceremony 15 tragedy 17 license 18 society 21 control Across: 2 march 4 paint 5 knowledge 6 worth 9 connection 10 sense 12 straw 13 supporters 14 beauty 16 challenge 18 speech 19 collection 20 cycle 22 exception

6 What fits together? a) abolish, analyse, benefit, communicate, contain, publish, refer, represent, suffer, vary **b)** 1 contain 2 reflect 3 published 4 suffer 5 represent 6 analyse 7 abolished 8 benefit 9 vary 10 communicate

7 Words without vowels: 1 James overcame his fear of heights and started hiking in the mountains. 2 Personally, I have never been to a rainforest. 3 Using plastic plates and straws is not environmentally friendly. 4 Australia is a multicultural society.

8 Word families: 1 amazing 2 pride 3 differ 4 identify 5 criminal 6 diversity 7 friendship 8 care

9 Word trios: a) 1 glas, plate, straw 2 phone, communicate, message 3 diversity, multicultural, society 4 environment, harm, pollution
b) (*Individuelle Lösungen; Lösungsvorschlag*) 1 Glass straws are a good alternative to plastic ones. 2 I use my phone to communicate and send messages. 3 A multicultural society is full of diversity. 4 Pollution causes a lot of harm to the environment.

10 Say it in English – talking about the environment: (*Individuelle Lösungen; Lösungsvorschlag*) 1 We must protect the beauty of nature. 2 The tropical rainforests are in danger. 3 Fish suffer from high water temperatures. 4 Plastic straws and plates are banned to protect the environment. 5 Lots of people protest the destruction of the environment. 6 Too much tourism, at beaches and on mountains for example, can destroy nature. 7 Climate change is the main cause of extreme weather. 8 Natural disasters like major flooding or tornados are happening more and more often. 9 It's still not too late to do something against climate change.

11 Connectives and conjunctions: a) 1 meanwhile 2 although 3 however 4 even though 5 as soon as 6 as if 7 after 8 although **b)** 1D 2F 3E 4B 5C 6A
c) (*Individuelle Lösungen; Lösungsvorschlag*) 1 I've drawn a picture so you can understand what it looks like. 2 We arrived at the cinema just as the film was starting. 3 Since you helped me, I'll give you an extra piece of cake. 4 I like apples whereas my friend likes pears. 5 Even though it was raining, we went on a walk. 6 We won't stop until we reach the finish line.

12 Phrases: gain experience, ban plastic, contains the necessary information, get back from school, specialize in a certain topic, overcome difficulties, attach a photo, learn a foreign language

13 Do you know the words? 1 harm – something that causes a bad situation or that damages something | Pollution causes harm to the environment.
2 license – an official document that allows you to do something | I don't have a driver's license but I will next year. 3 tragedy – something terrible, a really bad event | The car crash was a real tragedy. 4 exception – something that is different to the norm | The teacher made an exception for the boy who couldn't write. 5 rainforest – a tropical area covered in trees where it rains a lot | Rainforests are filled with lots of cool animals. 6 speech – a talk that is given in front of lots of people | I made a speech about my project in front of the whole class.

14 Check your vocab: 1 are related to 2 as 3 according to 4 is based on 5 overcame 6 possibly 7 just 8 despite 9 currently 10 contains 11 is floating 12 to take a risk 13 got back 14 sign up for 15 no matter 16 foreign 17 meanwhile 18 specializes 19 represents 20 runs

15 MY words – Australia: (*Individuelle Lösungen*)

Theme 2: Teenage life

1 Hidden phrases:

S	O	T	O	D	O	S	O	M	E	T	H	I	D	O	W	T	D	E	P	P	U	P	P	O
O	D	D	D	O	S	O	M	E	I	N	G	C	E	D	O	D	E	S	O	U	S	U	O	S
T	O	E	O	M	O	M	E	T	H	I	N	O	M	E	D	I	U	S	U	B	E	S	P	O
D	T	S	O	E	M	E	T	H	I	N	G	C	O	M	E	W	S	E	B	G	B	E	P	P
E	S	O	C	T	E	T	H	I	C	G	C	O	M	E	W	D	E	B	G	N	G	B	U	P
D	O	P	G	N	T	H	I	N	G	C	O	H	I	W	D	E	N	G	N	I	N	G	S	E
O	P	P	P	I	H	I	N	G	C	O	M	T	W	D	E	N	R	N	I	H	I	N	G	B
U	S	U	P	N	I	N	G	M	E	D	O	E	D	E	N	R	E	I	H	T	H	I	N	G
B	E	S	M	O	N	G	C	O	M	E	E	M	O	N	R	E	C	E	T	E	S	H	T	I
U	S	T	O	C	G	C	O	M	E	D	O	O	S	R	E	C	N	R	E	M	O	S	I	W
O	T	N	W	O	C	E	M	E	T	O	O	S	H	E	C	N	O	N	C	E	R	N	E	D
S	O	T	H	D	O	M	N	W	N	T	T	I	T	C	N	O	C	O	E	R	N	E	I	T
O	M	E	T	E	M	E	D	O	W	T	I	W	I	N	O	C	E	C	R	E	E	D	W	I
G	N	I	H	D	E	D	O	W	W	I	W	P	W	I	C	E	B	E	C	N	D	A	I	T
A	S	N	I	S	S	E	B	N	P	U	E	U	P	W	O	C	T	B	O	N	A	G	A	I
S	F	A	R	A	S	M	E	E	M	O	M	E	U	I	B	T	S	T	I	C	G	A	G	A
S	A	R	M	O	S	O	B	M	O	C	O	W	P	T	E	B	N	S	A	G	A	E	A	G
S	S	A	E	M	E	M	E	B	C	D	S	H	W	I	S	N	I	A	G	A	E	T	E	A
O	S	S	B	E	B	Y	D	E	N	E	H	T	I	S	N	I	A	G	A	E	T	A	T	A
C	Y	D	O	B	O	D	Y	N	R	D	S	H	T	H	I	A	G	A	E	T	A	N	I	N
S	I	Y	D	O	D	Y	N	R	E	M	O	S	H	M	D	G	D	I	S	C	R	I	M	A
C	S	I	Y	D	S	C	O	E	C	E	M	O	S	O	I	N	G	D	C	R	I	N	I	N
O	C	S	I	Y	I	S	C	O	N	C	E	M	O	M	H	I	D	I	R	I	M	I	N	A
N	O	C	S	I	S	C	C	N	C	E	I	E	M	E	T	H	I	D	I	M	I	N	E	T

1 be supposed to do something 2 come down to something 3 as far as somebody is concerned 4 come up with something 5 discriminate against 6 be concerned with something

b) 1 You're supposed to drink water every hour.
2 The decision comes down to what you want to do.
3 As far as I'm concerned, we should stay here.
4 We need to come up with a new idea. 5 We need to stop discriminating against people. 6 This chapter is concerned with teenage life.

2 In a debate: 1 as opposed to 2 raised 3 as I see it 4 in my opinion 5 claims 6 for my part 7 to be honest 8 I understand what you mean.

3 Missing letters: a) 1 communicate 2 appear 3 reveal 4 access 5 obsessive 6 self-esteem 7 addicted 8 sarcastic 9 misinformation 10 amused 11 humorous 12 specific **b)** 1 obsessive 2 humorous 3 specific 4 access 5 self-esteem 6 appeared 7 addicted 8 revealed

4 Nouns: 1 pie 2 drug, plot 3 issue, truth 4 button, shower 5 setting, subject 6 distance, majority 7 drugstore, breakdown 8 connection, calculator

5 Do you know the words? a) 1 hair 2 ear 3 mouth 4 head 5 brain 6 eye 7 nose 8 face **b)** 1 brain 2 ears 3 eyes 4 head 5 mouth 6 face 7 hair 8 nose

6 Paraphrasing: (*Lösungsvorschlag*) 1 This cake contains nuts. 2 There is so much information about the phone on this page, but I can't figure out where the price is. 3 I've never associated social media with addictions. 4 Matilda always tries to respond to her messages immediately. 5 Basketball appeals to Charlie because she loves to play in a team. 6 Theo didn't understand one word when he stared at the exercises. 7 The price of apples has varied a lot this week. 8 Riley relies on her bike to get to school.

7 Odd one out: a) 1 smart/schlau 2 by half/um die Hälfte 3 button/Knopf 4 solution/Lösung **b)** (*Lösungsvorschlag*) Because she was so smart, she knew all the answers. | He cut down his race time by half! | You have to push that button there. | We must find a solution to the problem.

8 Plural or no plural? a) smoking, attention, access, misinformation, bullying, self-esteem, body language **b)** writers, devices, sources, parties, conditions, cases, pharmacies, readers, illnesses, walls, extracts

5 Please forgive me for being late. I had transport trouble. 6 I would like to work at the shelter as I have a passion for helping animals. 7 I am a reliable person and am good at remembering details. 8 I look forword to hearing back from you.

7 Scrambled nouns: a) 1 device 2 ability 3 applicant 4 employer 5 involvement 6 qualification 7 rainforest 8 placement **b)** 1 placement 2 employer 3 qualification 4 device 5 involvement 6 applicant

8 Applying for a summer job: 1 in response 2 job advert 3 currently 4 native speaker 5 volunteer 6 responsible 7 feeding 8 have gained 9 suited for 10 reliable 11 willing 12 conservation

9 *Let, make* or *have*? 1 had 2 have 3 let 4 makes 5 make 6 let 7 let 8 had

10 Which is the right word? 1 essential 2 daily 3 features 4 whatever 5 unpredictable 6 potential 7 internship 8 average

11 Making opposites: un- believable, comfortable, friendly, motivated, predictable, realistic, reliable, sure dis- advantage, agree, appear, like in- capable, dependent, formal im- patient, polite

12 Say it in English – in a job interview: (*Individuelle Lösungen; Lösungsvorschlag*) 1 During the internship, I would like to gain experience in your company. 2 I am willing to work at the weekend. 3 I am creative and enjoy teamwork. 4 I am reliable and capable of coping with difficult tasks. 5 Applicants should be open to new challenges. 6 It is essential to be polite and friendly for the job. 7 Experience with editing texts is helpful but not necessary. 8 Thank you for your time and the interesting conversation. 9 I look forward to hearing from you.

13 A word puzzle: 1 enthusiastic 2 responsible 3 anonymous 4 characteristic 5 challenging 6 motivated 7 impolite 8 common 9 capable

14 Do you know the words? (*Lösungsvorschlag*) 1 native speaker – a person who speaks a language as their first language | Maria is a Italian native speaker. 2 cover letter – a letter you send as part of a job application | Don't forget to include a cover letter in your application. 3 conservation – the protection of nature and animals | National parks are important for the conservation of our planet. 4 ability – being able to do something | She has the ability to speak four languages. 5 furniture – things in house for example cupboards, chairs and tables | We need to buy some furniture for the new flat.

15 Make phrases: apply for an internship | be responsible for a project | be suited for a job | be willing to work long hours | cope with working under challenging conditions | gain valuable experience | get back to the applicant | look forward to hearing from you

16 Odd one out: a) 1 ability – Fähigkeit 2 stairs – Treppe 3 field – Feld 4 attention – Aufmerksamkeit 5 involvement – Beteiligung 6 placement – Praktikum **b)** (*Individuelle Lösungen; Lösungsvorschlag*) In my spare time, I like to practice my hobbies. Without free time, I'd be bored. | There's too much furniture in our house. There are five tables and six cupboards in the sitting room alone! | Technology has given us lots of devices. My favourite is the smartphone, but I also couldn't live without a TV. | All applicants should provide a CV. The successful candidate will be chosen based on this. | We would like a report that demonstrates your qualifications. We also ask for a reference to understand your previous work ethic. | Conservation is a way of protecting the environment. We can do this by not destroying the rainforest for example.

17 Word families: a) (*Lösungsvorschlag*) 1 able 2 behave 3 patient 4 collect 5 know 6 researcher 7 involved 8 apply **b)** 1 choose 2 creates 3 respond 4 differ ... from 5 editing 6 summarise 7 entertain 8 volunteer **c)** (*Lösungsvorschlag*) There is a lot of helpful information on the website. | The kids in the new class are really friendly. | Running and hiking requires a lot of movement.

18 Check your vocab: 1 requires 2 mention 3 responsible 4 essential 5 repeat 6 gained 7 cover letter 8 reliable 9 patience 10 at times 11 approve of 12 knowledge 13 cares for 14 works 15 panicked 16 count on me 17 sort 18 lacks 19 motivated 20 daily 21 involve 22 across

19 MY words – conversation: (*Individuelle Lösungen*)

6 Talking about texts: a) 1 perspective 2 rhetorical 3 plot 4 narrative 5 reader 6 quote 7 analyse 8 extract **b)** stylistic device

7 Say it in English – working with texts: (*Individuelle Lösungen; Lösungsvorschlag*) 1 The story is told from the perspective of a 15-year-old girl. 2 The characters are convincing and the plot is very exciting. 3 Different stylistic devices are used in the poem. 4 The novel describes how life on the coast has changed due to climate change. 5 The quote shows why the main character treated their best friend so badly in the situation. 6 The poet has written important poems about the problems of young people in the USA. 7 The first sentence already catches the reader's attention. 8 The narrative perspective swaps between the two main characters.

8 Adjectives and adverbs: a) 1 homeless 2 unexpected 3 armed 4 official 5 financial 6 capable 7 controversial 8 accidentally **b)** 1 unexpected 2 homeless 3 armed 4 controversial 5 accidentally 6 capable 7 financial 8 official

9 Words with similar meaning: a) fight – struggle | rise – increase | teach – educate | damage – harm | able – capable | immediate – direct | state – explain | current – existing **b)** 1 problem 2 conflict 3 over 4 follower 5 precious 6 fair

10 The Parkland shooting and *March for Our Lives*: 1 gun 2 laws 3 control 4 supporters 5 passed 6 measures 7 rise 8 controversial 9 politicians 10 weapon

11 Word game: (*Lösungsvorschlag*) P person protest political probably C case convince capable controversially T teacher tell terrible truthfully W word write wonderful wrongly

12 Word puzzle: a) 1 law 2 plot, gain 3 issue, means 4 safety, amount 5 witness, observe 6 attitude, struggle 7 rejection, guarantee 8 unemployed, unexpected **b)** 1 guarantee 2 gain 3 unexpected 4 attitude 5 witness 6 means

13 Which is the right word? 1 least 2 despite 3 just 4 forwards 5 such as

14 Check your vocab: 1 in fact 2 adopt 3 stated 4 such as 5 take into account 6 struggle 7 reflect 8 measures 9 least 10 first of all 11 related 12 are opposed to 13 controversial 14 repeat 15 have been dating 16 imitate 17 rejection 18 accidentally 19 was educated

15 MY words – expressing your opinion: (*Individuelle Lösungen*)

Theme 4: Chances and opportunities

1 Verbs – regular and irregular: a) assist, assisted, assisted, helfen | care for, cared for, cared for, sich kümmern um | fall over, fell over, fallen over, umfallen/hinfallen | feed, fed, fed, füttern | get started, got started, got/gotten started, anfangen | go wrong, went wrong, gone wrong, schiefgehen | hike, hiked, hiked, wandern | require, required, required, erfordern | run, ran, run, laufen/rennen/durchführen | set up, set up, set up, einrichten/gründen | store, stored, stored, lagern | suit sb/sth, suited sb/sth, suited sb/sth, zu jmd/etwas passen **b)** 1 required 2 went wrong 3 set up 4 fed 5 store 6 ran 7 assist 8 panicked 9 suits 10 gotten started

2 Wordsearch a)

Z	T	U	T	E	G	R	E	L	A	X	E	D	N
I	C	R	E	A	T	I	V	E	W	A	X	Y	A
Y	H	N	T	B	K	G	G	H	X	L	T	Z	E
E	N	T	H	U	S	I	A	S	T	I	C	R	S
C	V	F	O	A	B	T	Z	M	Q	L	A	X	S
B	R	K	J	W	T	I	D	Y	R	Z	Y	R	E
L	S	W	U	G	R	U	W	Y	C	B	W	F	N
B	N	T	Y	F	X	B	R	Q	Y	S	U	V	T
C	H	A	L	L	E	N	G	I	N	G	J	S	I
B	I	V	C	A	N	T	E	V	T	I	B	A	A
R	Z	Z	C	V	L	W	J	Q	F	H	E	X	L
U	S	R	E	S	P	O	N	S	I	B	L	E	Q
D	S	Y	Y	O	X	D	H	W	G	R	R	W	N
E	I	W	P	F	A	B	U	L	O	U	S	X	E

b) 1 essential 2 rude 3 tidy 4 responsible 5 enthusiastic 6 relaxed 7 fabulous 8 creative 9 challenging

3 Words without vowels: 1 We are looking for a reliable and motivated intern for our team. 2 You need to be willing to feed the animals every day. 3 Please, send your CV and all the references you might have. 4 You will gain a lot of experience during your internship.

4 Missing verbs: 1 store 2 assist with 3 collect 4 invests 5 repair 6 spread 7 act 8 mentioned

5 Phrases: a) approve of | assist in | come up with | cope with | count on | fall over | get back to | suited for **b)** 1 fell over 2 come up with 3 counting on 4 assisted … in 5 cope with 6 approve of 7 suited for 8 get back to

6 Job interview and cover letter: (*Lösungsvorschlag*) 1 I am a great communicator. 2 Computers aren't my strength but I am a fast learner. 3 I work well in a team. 4 Please could you repeat the question.

9 Scrambled words: a) 1 loving 2 thoughtful 3 smart 4 touching 5 gradually 6 humorous 7 sarcastic 8 rich **b)** 1 gradually 2 sarcastically 3 thoughtful 4 smart 5 humorous 6 richest

10 A cartoon: 1 Climate change is the main topic of the cartoon. 2 he appears to be … | his body language suggests … | His facial expression shows that … 3 (*Lösungsvorschlag*) body language: the way your body can reflect your feelings through leaning forward or raising the shoulders for example | facial expression: the way your face reflects your feelings when you smile for example 4 (*Individuelle Lösungen*)

11 A film review: a) 1F 2H 3B 4G 5C 6A **b)** (*Lösungsvorschlag*) 1 The film mainly appeals to a younger audience. 2 The end isn't very surprising and is rather boring. 3 The film's audience was hooked from the first moment. 4 All the actors are good, but the main actor was excellent. 5 The music made the film even scarier than it already is. 6 It's quite hard to follow the plot at the beginning. 7 I recommend the film to everyone who is interested in history. 8 Although the film doesn't have a happy ending, I liked it overall.

12 Mental health: 1 self-centered 2 illness 3 pharmacy 4 self-esteem 5 obsessive 6 anxious 7 breakdown 8 depressed

13 Verbs: a)

W	O	N	D	G	V	J	S	T	A	R	E	Y	W
M	A	P	P	E	A	R	V	Y	J	Y	F	T	Y
W	X	Z	V	Y	X	R	D	T	U	N	U	Y	E
S	D	R	X	R	E	S	P	O	N	D	V	D	E
V	E	Z	R	Q	L	Y	K	K	J	I	K	L	R
A	F	M	W	U	Z	E	D	E	L	E	T	E	C
O	I	Y	V	J	G	I	Y	V	S	T	C	D	R
F	N	F	B	A	N	A	L	Y	S	E	H	X	E
A	E	E	C	X	S	U	Q	T	F	P	L	P	N
D	W	I	D	C	O	N	C	L	U	D	E	Y	U
K	E	Q	N	P	G	T	K	G	I	J	J	P	T
P	O	K	R	E	J	E	C	T	P	P	U	S	H
A	C	E	D	C	L	Q	X	X	V	Y	P	R	X
E	R	A	I	S	E	L	H	C	L	A	I	M	T

b) 1 deleted 2 defined 3 rejected 4 stared 5 respond 6 pushed

14 More nouns: a) 1 brain 2 button 3 condition 4 misinformation 5 bullying 6 devices 7 walls 8 drug **b)** (*Individuelle Lösungen; Lösungsvorschlag*) I like to use my social media account to post pretty pictures. | Please may I go to the bathroom? | It is not possible to make an exception in this case. | I need to go to the drugstore to buy some medicine.

15 Phrases: 1E 2C 3H 4G 5B 6D 7A 8F

16 Check your vocab: 1 gradually 2 source 3 entirely 4 on purpose 5 despite 6 in particular 7 throughout 8 besides 9 figure out 10 by 11 in conclusion 12 personally 13 convey 14 convincing 15 by half 16 purpose 17 vary 18 attention 19 define 20 the … the 21 claims 22 extract 23 issue 24 truth

17 MY words – statistics: (*Individuelle Lösungen*)

Theme 3: Human rights for all?

1 What does it mean? a) identity – who or what somebody is attention – listening to, looking at or watching something carefully extract – a part of a text threat – when you tell somebody, you will harm them when they do not do what you want measure – an action which has a certain aim, e.g. to prevent something from happening supporter – a person who helps a party or a group of people motivation – why a person does something confrontation – a situation in which people are angry with each other because they have different opinions narrative – the description of a number of events society – people living together **b)** 1 extract 2 attention 3 confrontation 4 supporters 5 measures 6 threats **c)** 1 short extract 2 undivided attention 3 serious confrontation 4 active supporters 5 appropriate measures 6 terrible threats

2 Nouns, nouns, nouns: a) Across: 1 citizen 2 death 5 restriction 7 means 9 guarantee 12 constitution 14 harm 15 politician 18 association 22 attitude 23 march Down: 1 chart 3 weapon 4 rise 6 truth 7 military 8 belief 10 record 11 quote 13 speculation 16 doubt 17 measures 18 arms 19 silence 20 safety 21 laws **b)** 1 silent/silence 2 rise/arose 3 political/politician 4 safe/safety 5 beliefs/believe 6 speculate about/speculation 7 associate/association

3 *Cyber Teens* – an app against cyberbullying: a) 1 felt obliged 2 space 3 struggled 4 in fact 5 in addition 6 safety 7 were educated 8 impressive 9 aim **b)** (*Lösungsvorschlag*) 1 He wanted to provide a safe space and information for young people facing cyberbullying. 2 He organized internet safety classes and created local clubs. 3 It's the International Children's Peace Prize. 4 They have to be extremely involved in supporting the rights of children or improving the situation of children.

4 False friends: a) Meinung – opinion, meaning – Bedeutung | Note – grade/mark, note – Notiz | bekommen – get, become – werden | wer – who, where – wo | Lyrik – poetry, lyrics – Liedtext | also – so, also – auch **b)** 1 gym 2 don't have to 3 finally 4 grades/marks 5 where 6 phones/mobiles 7 are not allowed to 8 notes

5 Sentences:

1	2	3	4	5	6	7	8
D	G	C	B	H	A	F	E
g	f	d	h	e	b	c	a

Down ↓

1 a diagram
3 something that is used for fighting or attacking somebody
4 another word for an increase
6 "Please, tell me what really happened. Tell me the ..."
7 The ... is able to protect the country.
8 They have a strong ... in God.
10 Theo has a really good ... His grades and his behaviour are excellent.
11 Isa began her text with a ... from her favourite song.
13 There has been a lot of ... about the accident. Nobody really knew what had happened.
16 a feeling of not being sure or not believing something is true
17 We need to take more serious ... to protect the environment.
18 The people in the United States have the right to bear ...
19 No sound could be heard. There was absolute ...
20 This is too dangerous. We have to bring the people back home and back to ...
21 Japan has very strict gun ...

b) Complete the sentences. Use some of the words from the crossword and the following words from the same word families. Be careful to use the right from of the words, too.

arise • associate • believe • harm • political • quote • restrictive • safe • silent • speculate (on/about)

→ The text includes ___*quotes*___ from a Billie Eilish song.
___*Quote*___ from the text to illustrate how the characters feel.

1 Luna didn't know what to say so she remained ____________ but the ____________ felt very uncomfortable.

2 There was a ____________ in the number of shootings again. The question ____________ if the laws shouldn't be changed.

3 The Republicans and the Democrats are the two biggest ____________ parties in the USA.
Justin Trudeau is a Canadian ____________.

4 The library in school is a ____________ space for Noah. The ____________ of the participants is most important.

5 I do not share all your ____________ but I ____________ we can still be friends.

6 Please, don't ____________ the identity of the criminal. All this ____________ is not helpful.

7 Some people love to ____________ with famous people. *Organization* is another word for ____________.

3 *Cyber Teens* – an app against cyberbullying

a) Complete the text with the correct form of the words.

> Look up the words you don't know in an online dictionary. **!**

aim • educate • feel obliged • impressive • in addition • in fact • safety • space • struggle

ooo anappagainstcyberbullying

In 2019 Sadat Rahman from Bangladesh learned about a 15-year-old girl who had killed herself after a fake photo of her had been posted online. He was moved so much by her story that he **1** ______________ to do something and help other teenagers in his area. He created the app *Cyber Teens* as a safe **2** ______________ which offers information and help.

Over 300 children and teens who **3** ______________ with cyberbullying found support because they used Sadat's app. Fake social media accounts were reported and the teenagers were offered help when they had mental problems. **4** ______________, due to the app several people who had committed crimes online were caught by the police. **5** ______________ to the app Sadat organized internet **6** ______________ seminars and even created clubs in his area in all the schools where young people **7** ______________ on how to be safe online.

For this very **8** ______________ and valuable work, Sadat won the *International Children's Peace Prize* (*ICPP*) in 2020. The prize was introduced in 2005 by the *KidsRightsFoundation*. The foundation's **9** ______________ is to help protect children's rights all over the world. The *ICPP* is given annually to a child who fights for the protection of children's rights. Malala Yousafzai and Greta Thunberg are probably the best-known former winners. They won the prize in 2013 and 2019.

b) Read the text again and answer the questions.

1. Why did Salman create the app *Cyber Teens*?
2. What did he achieve with his activism?
3. What is the ICPP?
4. What does a child or teenager have to do to win the prize?

4 False friends

a) Complete the grid with the right German or English word.

> ! You will find a list of a number of *false friends* in your textbook on page 161.

German	correct English word	false English friend	correct German word
Meinung		meaning	
Note		note	
bekommen		become	
wer		where	
Lyrik		lyrics	
also		also	

b) Complete the sentences.

1 Jack goes to the ______________ (*Fitnessstudio*) every Friday.

2 You ______________ (*musst nicht*) come with me.

3 Two hours later than planned, we ______________ (*schließlich*) arrived at the hotel.

4 ______________ (*Wo*) did you leave the keys?

5 Please switch off your ______________ (*Handys*) and put them in your schoolbags.

6 Students ______________ (*nicht dürfen*) bring weapons to school.

5 Sentences

Match three parts to make sentences.

1 Evie always imitates	A signed up for	a the accident.
2 Ireland gained independence	B has adopted special drills	b the protest march.
3 Henry often forgets	C to respond to	c when the weather turned bad.
4 Almost every school in the USA	D her favourite singer	d the emails he receives.
5 The presentation	E to witness	e research in the internet.
6 A huge number of people	F down the mountain	f after three centuries of British rule.
7 We quickly retreated back	G on 18 April 1949	g and dresses like she does.
8 It was terrible	H involved a lot of	h to protect students from shootings.

1	2	3	4	5	6	7	8

6 Talking about texts

a) Find the words. Each number is a letter, e.g. the number 10 stands for the letter *O*.

1 A first-person narrator tells a story from his or her …

1	2	3	4	1	2	5	6	7	8	2

2 A question which does not need an answer is …

3	9	2	6	10	3	7	5	11	12
				o					

3 the main story of a film or book

1	12	10	6
		o	

4 A story can be told from different … perspectives.

14	11	3	3	11	6	7	8	2

5 a person who reads

3	2	11	15	2	3

6 sentences or parts of them that are taken from a text and repeated because they are useful or interesting

16	17	10	6	2
		o		

7 to study something, for example a text, in detail

11	14	11	12	18	19	2

8 a part of a text

2	13	6	3	11	5	6

1	2	3	4	5	6	7	8	9	10	11	12	13	14	15	16	17	18	19
									o									

b) Look at the letters in the blue boxes.
Can you find another word you need to talk about texts?
A rhetorical question is an example of a …

____

7 Say it in English – working with texts

Write down the German sentences in English.
Remember that you don't have to translate word for word.

> ! If you don't know the English words, you can always paraphrase the meaning in your own words.

1 Die Geschichte ist aus der Perspektive eines 15-jährigen Mädchens erzählt.

2 Die Figuren sind überzeugend und die Handlung ist sehr spannend.

3 In dem Gedicht werden verschiedene Stilmittel verwendet.

4 Der Roman erzählt, wie sich das Leben an der Küste durch den Klimawandel verändert hat.

5 Das Zitat zeigt, warum die Hauptfigur in der Situation ihren besten Freund so schlecht behandelt.

6 Die Dichterin hat wichtige Gedichte über die Probleme junger Menschen in den USA geschrieben.

7 Bereits der erste Satz weckt die Aufmerksamkeit der Leser.

8 Die Erzählperspektive wechselt zwischen den beiden Hauptfiguren.

8 Adjectives and adverbs

a) Complete the words with the missing vowels.

→ r__ __l__st__c__lly
1 h__m__l__ss
2 __n__xp__ct__d
3 __rm__d
4 __ff__c__ __l
5 f__n__nc__ __l
6 c__p__bl__
7 c__ntr__v__rs__ __l
8 __cc__d__nt__lly

b) Complete the sentences with the words from a). Use each word only once.

→ *Realistically*, we have to be really fast to still finish the task on time.

1 The end of the novel was completely __________.

2 After the flood hundreds of people were __________.

3 Heavily __________ policemen entered the school to stop the shooting.

4 The politician gave a very __________ speech.

5 In the USA in 2022 over 400 people were __________ killed by people with guns.

6 Most of the students were __________ of answering all the questions correctly.

7 When both parents lost their jobs, the whole family got in great __________ difficulties.

8 The __________ statistics show how many guns there are in the USA.

9 Words with similar meaning

a) Find the words that have a similar meaning and write them down.

rise	struggle	damage	able
immediate	fight	explain	teach
existing	educate	current	increase
harm	capable	state	direct

____
____
____
____
____
____

b) Look up words with a similar meaning and write them down.

1 issue __________
2 confrontation __________
3 across __________
4 supporter __________
5 valuable __________
6 just __________

10 The Parkland shooting and *March for Our Lives*

Complete the text. Be careful to use the correct form of the words.

control • controversial • gun • law • measures • pass • politician • rise • supporter • weapon

theparklandshootingandmarchforourlives

On 14 February 2018 a former student entered one of the buildings of Marjorie Stoneman Douglas Highschool carrying a rifle case and a backpack. He started to fire at students and teachers. Within only six minutes he had killed 17 people and harmed 17 others.

Only days after the shooting a group of students started *Never Again MSD* to protest against 1 ______________ violence and fight for stricter 2 ______________. Together with *Everytown for Gun Safety*, another group fighting for more gun 3 ______________, they organized a demonstration in Washington on 24 March 2018 called *March for Our Lives*.

Among the 4 ______________ of the march were celebrities such as Oprah Winfrey and Jimmy Fallon. Several hundred thousand people attended the march, the exact numbers being difficult to guess.

As a reaction to the protests of the Parkland students and the shooting, Florida 5 ______________ more restrictive laws and 6 ______________ which include a 7 ______________ in the minimum age for buying arms from 18 to 21 and a waiting period of three days before people can buy a gun. The measures were 8 ______________ though. Some 9 ______________ argued that they do not go far enough because there was no ban of certain types of 10 ______________ and they were critical of the decision to let staff bring guns to school.

11 Word game

Find words in each of the categories that start with the given letters and fill in the grid.

	a noun	a verb	an adjective	an adverb
R	*rival*	*regret*	*rich*	*roughly*
P				
C				
T				
W				

12 Word puzzle

a) Write down the English words. Be careful to write them down on the correct side.

							G	U	N	1										
										2		A								
								U		3										
										4			O							
					T					5										
						T				6										
										7				R						
							Y			8										

1 Gesetz – Waffen-
2 Handlung – bekommen, erreichen
3 Thema/Problem – Weg, Mittel, Art
4 Sicherheit – Menge
5 Zeuge – beobachten
6 Kampf – Haltung
7 Zurückweisung – Zusicherung
8 unerwartet – arbeitslos

b) Complete the sentences with some of the words from a).

1 There is no ____________ that people will keep their weapons in a secure place at home.

2 We won't ____________ much from these measures, as they are not strict enough.

3 The film's success was completely ____________.

4 It is sometimes difficult to keep a positive ____________ towards life.

5 There was no ____________ when the accident happened.

6 I don't have the financial ____________ to go on a long holiday every year.

13 Which is the right word?

Complete the sentences.

despite • forwards • just • least • such as

1 We need to take the ____________ expensive way to travel from New York to Texas.

2 William managed to arrive at school on time ____________ getting up so late.

3 It was difficult to make a ____________ decision.

4 Only a few people came ____________ when the teacher asked for volunteers.

5 Measures to reduce gun violence, ____________ background checks, are extremely important.

14 Check your vocab

Fill in the right words. Be careful to use the right form and use each word only once.

accidentally • adopt • be opposed to • controversial • educate • date • first of all • imitate • in fact • least • measure • reflect • rejection • related • repeat • state • struggle • such as • take into account

1 Luna searched for her phone everywhere when ______________ it was on her desk the whole time.

2 This doesn't work. We need to ______________ a different strategy to solve the problem.

3 The authors ______________ their opinion quite clearly.

4 Everybody has equal rights, ______________ the right to have an opinion or a belief.

5 We need to ______________ that this is a complicated task. It will take a while to complete it.

6 In many countries people ______________ against war, discrimination or hunger.

7 Find quotes that ______________ how the main character feels about the situation.

8 Despite new safety ______________, the number of accidents has increased again.

9 It will be ______________ likely to rain on Saturday. Let's go for a hike then.

10 ______________, read the text and look up all the words you don't understand.

11 The high number of deaths is directly ______________ to the high number of guns.

12 Too many politicians ______________ stricter gun-laws so there will be no or only small changes.

13 Measures against climate change are a ______________ topic.

14 You need to ______________ the phrases and their meaning a few times to be able to remember them.

15 Gianni and Miles ______________ for three months now. They are really happy.

16 Can you ______________ your favourite singer's voice?

17 Dan experienced a lot of ______________ when he and his family became homeless.

18 It is horrible how many children in the USA are ______________ shot every year.

19 Liam ______________ at a boarding school in Wales before he went to university in England.

15 MY words – expressing your opinion

On this page you can collect words and phrases you can use to express your opinion.
You can always come back later and add more words to it.

stating your opinion	agreeing or disagreeing
For me, it is obvious…	*I completely agree …*

summarizing your opinion

All things considered …

1 Verbs – regular and irregular

a) Fill in the grid with the correct forms of the verbs and the German translation.

infinitive	simple past	past participle	German
assist			
care for			
fall over			
feed			
get started			
go wrong			
panic			
require			
run			
set up			
store			
suit sb/sth			

b) Complete the sentences with some of the verbs from a). Be careful to use the right form of the words and use each word only once.

! You can look up irregular verbs in your textbook on pages 283-285.

1 The task was difficult. It ________________ a lot of attention.

2 The cake tastes really bad. I have no idea what ________________.

3 Amir and Lia ________________ a new youth club last month.

4 The cat looks really hungry. Have you ________________ her yet?

5 We need to ________________ these books somewhere.

6 Joshua and Amelia ________________ a theatre club at their school last year.

7 Volunteers will ________________ with the cleaning of the beach.

8 All the horses ________________ when they heard the fireworks.

9 The dress you wore yesterday really ________________ you.

10 Just when I thought that I had finally ________________ with my homework, my dog wanted to go out.

2 Wordsearch

a) Find nine adjectives in the wordsearch. Circle them. → ↓

Z	T	U	T	E	G	R	E	L	A	X	E	D	N
I	C	R	E	A	T	I	V	E	W	A	X	Y	A
Y	H	N	T	B	K	G	G	H	X	L	T	Z	E
E	N	T	H	U	S	I	A	S	T	I	C	R	S
C	V	F	O	A	B	T	Z	M	Q	L	A	X	S
B	R	K	J	W	T	I	D	Y	R	Z	Y	R	E
L	S	W	U	G	R	U	W	Y	C	B	W	F	N
B	N	T	Y	F	X	B	R	Q	Y	S	U	V	T
C	H	A	L	L	E	N	G	I	N	G	J	S	I
B	I	V	C	A	N	T	E	V	T	I	B	A	A
R	Z	Z	C	V	L	W	J	Q	F	H	E	X	L
U	S	R	E	S	P	O	N	S	I	B	L	E	Q
D	S	Y	Y	O	X	D	H	W	G	R	R	W	N
E	I	W	P	F	A	B	U	L	O	U	S	X	E

b) Complete the sentences with the words from the wordsearch.

1 For this job experience in video editing is ____________.

2 It is ____________ to not apologize for being late.

3 Max likes to keep his room ____________.

4 Joon will be ____________ for the photos we need for our presentation.

5 Levy really wants the job because he is so ____________ about creating computer games.

6 It is not easy to be ____________ in a job interview.

7 Sadie is our ____________ new cook! Her food always tastes fantastic.

8 We need a ____________ person for this project who is able to come up with exciting new ideas.

9 Working as a teacher can be very ____________.

3 Words without vowels

1 We are l___ ___k___ng for a r___l___ ___bl___ and m___t___v___t___d ___nt___rn for our team.

2 You n___ ___d to be w___ll___ng to f___ ___d the ___n___m___ls every day.

3 Pl___ ___s___ send your CV and all the r___f___r___nc___s you m___ght have.

4 You will g___ ___n a lot of ___xp___r___ ___nc___ during your ___nt___rnsh___p.

4 Missing verbs

Complete the sentences with the correct form of the verbs written in /…/.

1 There is so much stuff in my room! I don't know where to ______________ /stɔː/ it anymore.

2 Finn needs to ______________ /əˈsɪst wɪð/ feeding the animals today.

3 Don't forget to ______________ /kəˈlekt/ the book you have ordered.

4 Ivy ______________ /ɪnˈvest/ a lot of time in her hobbies.

5 Can you ______________ /rɪˈpeə/ my bike?

6 Nasir had ______________ /spred/ the books he needed for his presentation on his desk.

7 Interns will ______________ /ækt/ as park representatives and answer questions.

8 You never ______________ /ˈmenʃ(ə)n/ that you can speak four languages. That's awesome!

5 Phrases

a) Make eight phrases with the verbs and the prepositions and write them down. Use each preposition only once.

approve • assist • come • cope • count • fall • get back • suited

for • in • of • on • over • to • up with • with

____

____

b) Complete the sentences with the correct form of the phrases from a).

1 Archie badly hurt himself when he ran down the stairs and ______________ his dog last week.

2 We still need to ______________ a really good idea for our party next week.

3 You have to help me with this, I absolutely ______________ you!

4 Yesterday Aaliyah ______________ Luca ______________ writing his cover letter.

5 I am not sure if I can ______________ the noise for very much longer.

6 The company will probably ______________ your experience in editing.

7 People who don't like to talk to strangers will not be ______________ this job.

8 I will ______________ you when I have bought the tickets for the concert.

6 Job interview and cover letter

Rewrite the sentences. Use phrases which are appropriate in a job interview or in a cover letter.

1 I love to talk about myself.

____

2 Don't know much about computers but I'm always willing to learn.

____

3 My friends say that I'm a good team player.

____

4 Huh? Why do you want to know that?

____

5 Sorry I'm late. I couldn't find my bus ticket.

____

6 I want the job at the shelter because I absolutely love all animals. They're so cute!

____

7 I am so reliable. I never forget anything.

____

8 Can't wait to hear from you guys.

____

7 Scrambled nouns

a) Find the words and write them down.

1 CEVIDE ______________

2 TYABILI ______________

3 ANTLICAPP ______________

4 ERPLOYEM ______________

5 MENLVEVOTIN ______________

6 FILICAQUAONTI ______________

7 RAIESTFORN ______________

8 ENTCEMPLA ______________

b) Match some of the words from a with the definitions below.

1 a person who formally asks for a job or an internship: ______________

2 a person or a company who pays people who work for them: ______________

3 a special skill or an education which is needed for a job: ______________

4 the act of taking part in something: ______________

8 Applying for a summer job

Complete the letter. Be careful to write down the correct form of the verbs.

conservation • currently • feed • gain • in response • job advert • native speaker • reliable • responsible • suit • volunteer • willing

Dear Sir/Madam,

I am writing 1 ________________ to the 2 ________________ on your website. 3 ________________, I am in my last year at school. I am a German 4 ________________ and also speak English fluently. In my spare time I regularly 5 ________________ at the local animal rescue shelter. I am 6 ________________ for 7 ________________ the cats and dogs and also have contact with visitors. Because of the experiences I 8 ________________ there, I am convinced that I would be 9 ________________ for the job.

I am a 10 ________________ person and 11 ________________ to work hard. For many years the 12 ________________ of nature has been very important to me.

I look forward to hearing from you.

Yours faithfully,

Leon Schumacher

9 *Let, make or have?*

Complete the sentences with the correct form of *let*, *make* or *have*.

Need help with the task?
You can look up the use of *let*, *make* and *have* in your textbook on page 192.

1 It was a great help for Mr Wilkins that he ________________ somebody care for him when he was ill.

2 Emma needs to ________________ her hair cut.

3 Finally, the principal ________________ the students set up a youth club.

4 Henry hates answering the phone but his brother always ________________ him do it.

5 Don't ________________ me hike across this mountain!

6 It is quite late already. Please, ________________ me get back to you tomorrow.

7 Would you ________________ me help you with the task?

8 The teacher ________________ the class tidied by the students.

10 Which is the right word?

Write down the right word.

1 Experience in working with small children is ____________ for the internship. (essential/special)

2 My ____________ responsibilities include opening the café and cleaning the tables. (daily/tidy)

3 Rory's new smartphone has some great ____________. (features/points)

4 ____________ you decide, I will support you. (nothing/whatever)

5 At the coast the weather can be very ____________. (well-known/unpredictable)

6 ____________ applicants should be willing to work on Sundays as well. (potential/possible)

7 Alexis gained valuable experience during her ____________ at the shelter. (internship/activity)

8 Your ____________ working day will start at 8 o'clock in the morning. (majority/average)

11 Making opposites

Match the words with the correct prefix to make opposites. Write them down in the grid. When you are not sure, you can look up the words in a dictionary.
You can write down your own words, too.

Make your vocabulary even bigger by learning a word and its opposite at the same time.

advantage • agree • appear • believable • capable • comfortable • dependent • formal • friendly • like • motivated • patient • polite • predictable • realistic • reliable • sure

un-	dis-	in-	im-

12 Say it in English – in a job interview

Write down the sentences in English.

Remember that you don't have to translate word for word. Check your textbook on pages 201-202 for helpful words or phrases.

1 Ich möchte während des Praktikums Erfahrungen in Ihrem Unternehmen sammeln.

2 Ich bin dazu bereit auch an den Wochenenden zu arbeiten.

3 Ich bin kreativ und arbeite gerne in einem Team.

4 Ich bin zuverlässig und in der Lage schwierige Aufgaben zu bewältigen.

5 Die Bewerber sollten offen für neue Herausforderungen sein.

6 Für den Job ist es unverzichtbar immer höflich und freundlich zu sein.

7 Erfahrung im Bearbeiten von Texten ist hilfreich aber nicht notwendig.

8 Vielen Dank für Ihre Zeit und das interessante Gespräch.

9 Ich freue mich darauf von Ihnen zu hören.

13 A word puzzle

Do the word puzzle and then write down the solution.

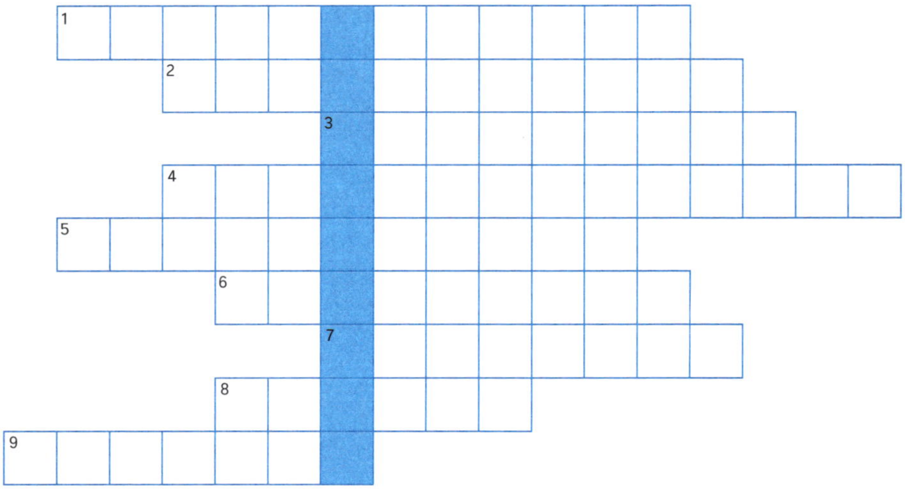

1 Tom is a great fan of the band Stray Kids. He is totally ... about them.
2 You will be ... for entertainment of the guests.
3 Please, delete the name and address. The letter has to be ...
4 Patience is a highly valued ... for working with people.
5 Starting a new job is ... experience, but I am sure you'll manage.
6 Emma was highly ... to volunteer in the museum as she is really interested in history.
7 It is rude and very ... to let other people wait for you.
8 So many people are nervous before a job interview. It's a very ... thing.
9 I would be right for the job because I am ... of working in a team.

14 Do you know the words?

Fill in the grid.

		your own definition of the word	a sentence with the word
→	field	*A field can be an area of land where grass or other plants grow.*	*The farm is surrounded by fields.*
1	native speaker		
2	cover letter		
3	conservation		
4	ability		
5	furniture		

15 Make phrases

Write down eight phrases. Use all the words only once.

apply for • be responsible for • be suited for • be willing to • cope with • gain • get back to • look forward to

an internship • hearing from you • a job • a project • the applicant • valuable experience • work long hours • working under challenging conditions

16 Odd one out

a) Find the odd one out. Circle it and write down the German translation.

→ job ad • cover letter • patience • internship — *Geduld*

1 spare time • ability • hobby • free time

2 furniture • table • cupboard • stairs

3 field • device • smartphone • TV

4 CV • applicant • attention • candidate

5 report • reference • qualification • involvement

6 placement • rainforest • conservation • environment

b) Write one or two sentences with the three words that belong together.

I need to write a cover letter for the internship at the zoo. The job ad for it sounds really exciting.

17 Word families

a) Look at the nouns on the left. Complete the grid with another word from the same word family. It can be a verb, an adjective, an adverb or another noun.

Words from the same word family often have very similar meanings. That makes it easier to guess the meaning of words you don't know. **!**

→	art	*artist*
1	ability	
2	behaviour	
3	patience	
4	collection	
5	knowledge	
6	research	
7	involvement	
8	application	

b) Complete the sentences with another word from the same word family.

1 That's a difficult choice. Can you help me to ______________?

2 Elijah is a really creative person. He always ______________ the best videos.

3 Lily smiled in response when she heard the result of her test. Don't forget to ______________ your emails.

4 There is no big difference between the two apples. They don't ______________ much ______________ each other.

5 Theo still has to edit his text. It will be much better after ______________.

6 Don't write a summary of the whole book. Just ______________ the main ideas.

7 The show was very entertaining. Jack loves to ______________ other people.

8 There were a lot of volunteers cleaning up the beach. Many of them like to ______________ regularly.

c) Look at the words. Find other words from the same family and write down your own sentences.

help • friend • move

____

____

18 Check your vocab

Fill in the right words. Be careful to write down the correct form of the words.

across • approve of • at times • care for • count on sb/sth • cover letter • daily • essential • gain • involve • lack • knowledge • motivated • mention • panic • patience • reliable • repeat • require • research • responsible • sort • work

1 The job ______________________ experience with editing.

2 Working with people often requires a lot of ______________________.

3 Today the interns will be ______________________ for feeding the horses.

4 It is absolutely ______________________ that the applicant can speak Spanish.

5 Could you please ______________________ the question? I did not quite understand it.

6 I ______________________ a lot of experience during the placement last month.

7 The ______________________ needs to be written in formal language.

8 The company is looking for a ______________________ person.

9 Did you ______________________ the author of the article?

10 ______________________ the job can be exhausting because there is so much work to do.

11 The teacher needs to ______________________ our topic for the presentation.

12 Your ______________________ of English literature is amazing.

13 Junu always ______________________ Theo's hamster when Theo is on holiday.

14 Can you show me how this ______________________?

15 Ava ______________________ when her dog suddenly ran across the street.

16 I will help you. You can ______________________ me!

17 ______________________ the phrases into the grid.

18 The applicant ______________________ the necessary experience.

19 We are looking for hard-working and highly ______________________ volunteers.

20 Experiencing ______________________ working life can be a great help if you want to find out which job you like to do.

21 It's a good idea to ______________________ more people in the organization of the march.

22 Ezra has to drive ______________________ the whole town to get to soccer training.

19 MY words – conversation

On this page you can collect all the words and phrases you can use in a conversation.

! You can always come back later and add more words or phrases.

asking for clarification

Could you please repeat your question?

keeping a conversation running

That sounds really interesting.

beginning and ending a conversation

It has been great talking to you.